THE SLEEPY HOLLOW MYSTERY

created by
GERTRUDE CHANDLER WARNER

Illustrated by Anthony VanArsdale

Albert Whitman & Company
Chicago, Illinois

Library of Congress Cataloging-in-Publication
data is on file with the publisher.

Copyright © 2015 by Albert Whitman & Company
Published in 2015 by Albert Whitman & Company

ISBN 978-0-8075-2843-3 (hardcover)
ISBN 978-0-8075-2844-0 (paperback)

THE BOXCAR CHILDREN® is a registered
trademark of Albert Whitman & Company.

Printed in the United States of America
10 9 8 7 6 5 4 3 2 1 LB 20 19 18 17 16 15

Illustrated by Anthony VanArsdale

For more information about Albert Whitman & Company,
visit our web site at www.albertwhitman.com.

Contents

CHAPTER 1

Sleepy Hollow

The Haunted Hollow Gift Shop, located on the first floor of a big yellow house with white shutters, was completely dark when Mrs. McGregor parked the car in front of it.

"I thought Mrs. Vanderhoff was expecting us," Jessie Alden said, peering out the car window.

"She is," said Mrs. McGregor, the Alden's housekeeper. "I'm not surprised the shop is dark, since it's closed at night, but the lights in the upstairs apartment should be on."

Ten-year-old Violet Alden rolled down the car window and leaned out. "I think there's someone standing on the porch. It looks like a man in a cape, but he's standing very still."

Their dog, Watch, perched on Jessie's lap, began to growl.

The youngest Alden, Benny, asked, "Can I see?" He stuck his head out and then jerked back in, bumping against Violet. "Roll up the window, quick! The man doesn't have a head. It's there on the ground!"

His older brother, Henry, took a flashlight out of the glove compartment. "It's probably some sort of Halloween decoration." He shone the light on the front of the shop. "It's a scarecrow. He's headless, all right, but the thing on the ground is just a carved pumpkin."

Benny moved closer to Jessie. "The town of Sleepy Hollow is already turning out to be spooky."

"There *is* something strange about that pumpkin head," Violet said. "It's all white."

"Is it a ghost pumpkin?" Benny asked.

"I've seen white pumpkins at farm stands,"

Jessie told him. "Some people like them because they're unusual."

"I think I like the orange ones better," Benny declared. "No ghost pumpkins for me."

"Are we sure this the right day?" Violet asked. "Maybe Mrs. Vanderhoff thought we were coming a different day."

"No, I just talked to Gretchen on Tuesday. I told her your fall break started this Friday," Mrs. McGregor said. The Aldens' grandfather was away on a business trip, so Mrs. McGregor had brought them to the Hudson River Valley to visit one of her old friends, Mrs. Vanderhoff. The children were excited to see how the town of Sleepy Hollow celebrated Halloween, and they were looking forward to going on one of the new ghost tours run by Mrs. Vanderhoff's daughter.

Henry Alden snapped on Watch's leash and got out of the car with the dog. "Why don't we ring the doorbell?"

The rest of them followed.

"The apartment door is on the side of the building," Mrs. Vanderhoff said.

Before they could ring the bell, a figure carrying a lantern came out of the shadows between the buildings. Violet, who was in front, let out a little squeak of surprise and took a step back.

"Don't be frightened," a woman's voice called. As she came forward, the lantern light showed a woman about Mrs. McGregor's age.

"Gretchen!" Mrs. McGregor exclaimed. "We were worried when we didn't see any lights. Children, this is my dear friend Mrs. Vanderhoff."

Mrs. Vanderhoff said, "I'm delighted to meet you. Now let me guess who is who. I've heard so much about you."

"Guess me first! Please!" Benny raised his hand.

"Hmmm...well, I know Henry is fourteen years old. Are you Henry?" She smiled when she said this to Benny and the older children knew she was teasing.

"No." Benny laughed. "I'm only six."

"Then you must be Benny, and the taller boy must be Henry."

"You're right!" Benny said. "Can you guess

the girls?"

Mrs. Vanderhoff smiled again. "The girls are easier to guess because I've heard Violet likes purple and I see one of you has on a purple sweater."

Violet nodded.

"I also know you're an artist," Mrs. Vanderhoff continued. "I hope you brought your paints! The Hudson River Valley is a famous spot for painting."

"I did bring them," Violet said. "I would like to try to paint some of the trees with their fall colors."

Mrs. Vanderhoff turned to Violet's sister. "So you must be Jessie," she said, shaking Jessie's hand. "And I'd recognize Watch anywhere." She patted the dog, and the terrier wagged his tail. "I'm sorry it's so dark, but the power is out," she explained.

"The dark made your porch look scary," Benny said.

"We thought the scarecrow was a headless man," Violet added.

Mrs. Vanderhoff looked puzzled. "The scarecrow isn't supposed to be scary. My

daughter Annika carved a happy face on the pumpkin head."

"The pumpkin head is on the ground," Jessie said. Henry shone the flashlight so Mrs. Vanderhoff could see it.

"Oh, that's too bad. The pumpkin must have fallen off the scarecrow frame. Annika wouldn't make a headless scarecrow. She doesn't like scary Halloween decorations. We'll fix the scarecrow tomorrow. Now, if you want to bring your suitcases around back, I do have a nice fire going in the fire pit. I also have some hot cider for everyone. My other daughter Margot made some crullers today too. I think you will like those."

"I don't know what crullers are, but they sound good!" Benny said. "I'm hungry."

Mrs. Vanderhoff laughed. "Crullers are a special kind of doughnut dipped in sugar. The recipe has been in my family for generations, ever since the first Dutch settlers came to this area of New York."

"We can't wait to try them," Jessie said as she helped Henry get the suitcases out of the car.

Henry paused to look around. "The power isn't out anywhere else," he said. "That restaurant next door has all its lights on."

Mrs. Vanderhoff sighed. "The restaurant is the reason we don't have electricity. They are doing some repair work. Somehow the power to my property was cut off. It's supposed to be fixed in the morning, but until then, we'll have to rely on flashlights and candles."

A paved path led to a fenced-in backyard. Torches in the ground lit a stone patio with a fire pit in the center. The fire in it blazed away. Jessie thought it looked very cozy, like a little island of light in the dark yard.

"Take a seat," Mrs. Vanderhoff said, motioning to the benches placed around the fire. They all sat down except Watch, who stood next to Henry. The dog sniffed the air and then whined.

"Settle down, Watch," Henry said. He patted the dog, who sat down but continued to look around, his ears alert.

"Who would like hot cider?" Mrs. Vanderhoff asked.

"I would!" Benny said.

"I think we all would," Mrs. McGregor added.

Mrs. Vanderhoff went over to a small table that held a thermos, mugs, a large platter covered with foil, and a cookie jar. As she poured, she explained, "Annika will be back with her ghost-tour guests very soon. They walk most of the way, but then a friend of hers picks them up in an old wagon and brings them back here. When they arrive, everyone sits around the fire for snacks and one last story."

"How is the ghost-tour business going?" Mrs. McGregor asked.

Mrs. Vanderhoff handed a mug of cider to Benny. "Annika is just starting out so it's been a little slow. Her tours are unusual. She's calling them family-friendly ghost walks. So many young children think some parts of Halloween are too scary. She tells interesting stories and shows them some beautiful places in the woods."

"That's a good idea," Violet said. "Sometimes I'm scared of the dark. My friends like Halloween haunted houses, but I don't."

"Annika is hoping some of the people who take the tours will tell their friends," Mrs. Vanderhoff said. "Every little bit of money helps. My poor old house needs so many repairs. We fix one thing just when something else breaks."

"If you have some tools I can use," Henry said, "I'll be happy to fix what I can. I like to fix things."

"Thank you, Henry. I have several small jobs you could do. At least the apartment over the garage where you'll be staying is in good shape, except it doesn't have any power at the moment. If you are too frightened to stay out there, we can all stay inside the main house."

"We'll be fine," Jessie said. "We're used to staying in places without electricity. Our boxcar in the woods didn't have any power."

After their parents died, the Alden children had run away. They had never met their grandfather, but they were afraid of him because they'd heard he was mean. The children had found an abandoned boxcar in the woods and made it their home. When their grandfather found them, they realized he wasn't mean at all. He brought them to his home to live with him and Mrs. MacGregor. He even had the boxcar moved to his backyard.

Mrs. Vanderhoff's cell phone rang. She answered and a serious look appeared on her face. "Oh dear. Margot isn't home, but I'll be there right away." Putting the phone away, she said, "That was Annika. Her friend Isiah didn't show up with the wagon and she can't reach him. I need to go pick up the tour group and bring them back here."

"Will everyone fit in your car?" Mrs. McGregor asked. "I can take my car too."

"Thank you. I was going to have to take two trips," Mrs. Vanderhoff said. "You children will be fine here by yourselves for a little while, won't you?"

"I guess so. You'll be back soon, right?" Benny asked. "It is very dark even with the fire."

Jessie put her arm around him. "We'll be fine," she assured him. But she looked around at the trees with their twisted branches looming over the yard and hoped they wouldn't have to stay alone for *too* long.

"Have a cruller or a cookie while you're waiting." Mrs. Vanderhoff motioned to the covered platter and the cookie jar. "There are plenty."

After Mrs. Vanderhoff and Mrs. McGregor left, Jessie finished pouring the cider for everyone and asked, "Which do you want, cookies or crullers?" She tried to sound cheerful so the others wouldn't realize she was already getting a little spooked about being in such a dark, strange place.

"I think we should try something new, so I vote for the crullers," Henry said.

Jessie passed them out. "I like the shape of these. They look like someone braided pieces of dough."

"These are yummy," Violet said, biting into hers. "They're so much crunchier that regular doughnuts."

"I like the sugar that's all over them!" Benny said.

"Maybe I can get the recipe from Mrs.

Vanderhoff," Jessie said. "I can try to make them."

The wind picked up and the branches of the trees rustled. Most of them had already lost their leaves, but a few fell from a big oak tree and blew onto the patio. Watch leaped up and tried to catch some.

"I'm glad we have a fire." Jessie shivered, buttoning the top button of her coat. "It's chilly." The moving branches of the trees threw shadows on the ground, and they looked like broken skeletons dancing in the circle of light from the fire.

Just then Violet jumped, spilling some of her drink on the ground.

Henry was so startled, he almost dropped his drink too. "Violet! What's wrong?"

"Did you hear that noise?"

CHAPTER 2

A Headless Horseman

Henry said, "I don't hear anything but the wind." He listened and for a moment though he heard a low rumble of thunder coming from down the street. It stopped, and he decided his ears must have been playing tricks on him.

"I don't hear anything either," Jessie said.

Violet was quiet for a moment and then asked, "You didn't hear anything that sounded sort of like an animal snorting, did you?"

Benny made pig noises and then asked,

"You mean like that?" Henry and Jessie laughed.

"No, not like that," Violet said. "It's hard to explain. Listen again."

They all sat quietly again, but there were no noises except the wind and the leaves blowing across the patio. Watch had stopped chasing them. He sat next to Henry with his ears alert.

"I still don't hear anything," Jessie said.

"Me neither." Benny took another bite of his cruller.

"I guess I imagined it." Violet scooted her bench closer to the fire.

Watch got up and walked toward the edge of the patio. He pulled on the end of the leash in Henry's hands.

"I think you can let go of his leash," Jessie said. "He can't get outside the fence." As soon as Henry let go, Watch slunk down on his belly. He crept over to the side of the yard growling softly.

"That's the direction I heard the noise," Violet whispered.

"Watch, what do you see?" Henry got up

and walked over to the fence. He shined the flashlight into the area behind the café next door. "I don't see anything. Silly Watch. It's just the wind." He listened for the thunder sound, and for an instant he thought he heard it again. It stopped, so he came back and sat down. They all huddled around the fire, which no longer seemed as bright.

Soon after, they heard the sound of cars, and then voices as a group of people came into the back yard.

Jessie was relieved to hear Mrs. Vanderhoff's voice. "The tour group is back!" Jessie told the others.

A young woman wearing a red velvet cape and carrying a lantern led the group to the patio. "Welcome to our house," she said. Even though she was smiling, her voice was a little shaky. Her wavy blond hair was falling out of the bun on top of her head.

She smiled at the Aldens, said hello, and told her group, "These are friends of the family. Why don't you all sit down and I'll serve you some treats." There were two sets of parents and three children in the group, but none of them looked like they were having fun.

The oldest child was girl about Benny's age and she was wearing a pretty princess costume, but Violet thought the girl was the most unhappy-looking princess she had ever seen. A little boy about two or three years old was dressed as a dragon. As the group walked to the patio, the boy grabbed hold of his father's leg and hid his face.

"We can help," Violet said, jumping up. Mrs. Vanderhoff handed her the cookie jar. Violet pulled the lid off and offered the jar to the third child, a little girl dressed like a mouse, who had sat down in the spot next to Violet's.

The girl reached her hand in and then jerked it back out. She screamed, "Gross! It's full of something yucky. I think there are worms and dirt in there."

Violet peered into the cookie jar. "It does have something in it besides cookies," she said. She sniffed it. "It doesn't smell like dirt though."

Jessie came over. "Can I look?" Violet

held it out to her and Jessie looked inside. "It smells like chocolate and some sort of fruit smell." She reached her hand in and pulled out something sticky. "This isn't really a worm. It's gummy candy meant to look like a worm. And I think the dirt is just crushed up chocolate cookies. We had treats like this at school last year for Halloween."

She looked at Mrs. Vanderhoff, who looked at Annika.

Annika said, "I don't know how those got in there. I filled the jar up with cookies myself."

"I guess it's a joke," Henry said.

"It's not a funny joke," the little girl's mother said as she took her daughter's hand. "This ghost tour is not turning out the way we expected."

"I'm sorry," Annika said. "I don't know who would play a trick like that."

A shriek rang out from the alley. It sounded like an angry scream.

Everyone stood up. A horse neighed, and they could hear hooves pounding. Watch began to bark. The boy dressed as a dragon cried out and his father picked him up. The Aldens and Annika ran to the fence at the back of the yard. The rest of the group but the scared toddler and his father followed them. They saw a big black horse come rushing down the alley. The horse's rider wore a black cape that billowed out in the wind.

"There's something not right about the rider," Violet said.

Henry shone the flashlight at the person on the horse.

"The rider doesn't have a head!" Benny cried. They all jumped back in surprise.

As the horse passed by the fence, the rider took something from inside the cape and held it up.

It resembled a head with glowing teeth and eyes. The rider heaved the head toward the group.

They all dodged away, bumping into one another. It landed with a thud in front of them. It split open, spraying them all with thick red liquid.

All three of the children from the tour group begin to sob.

"Don't cry," Jessie said. "It was just a pumpkin.."

One of the mothers held out her hands, which were speckled with red. "It looks like blood!"

Violet held out one of the pieces of the pumpkin. It was coated on the inside with the red liquid. "That's not blood. It's paint. I

can smell it." She turned it over. "And look at this on the outside that looks like an eye. It's glow-in-the-dark paint."

The woman said to Annika, "Young lady, that was a terrible trick. You advertise this as a ghost tour for families, but look at all the children crying. This was far too frightening. They'll have nightmares tonight."

"I'm so sorry," Annika said. "That horseman was not part of the tour. I don't know who it was, or why he would do something like that."

The woman took hold of her children's hands. "I don't believe some headless horseman from a story just happened to show up to throw a pumpkin at us. I will not be recommending this tour to any of our friends. In fact, I'm going to post a review online. People should know this is not for families. Let's go, everyone."

After the group left, Annika looked like she was going to cry. Mrs. Vanderhoff put her arm around her daughter's shoulders. "I'm sorry about the awful trick."

Henry picked up another piece of the

pumpkin. "This is another one of those strange pumpkins. It's white, just like the ones in front."

"I use white pumpkins for the logo of my ghost-tour business," Annika said. "Whoever played this trick must have used a white pumpkin on purpose. They aren't easy to find."

"I wonder if the same person put the cookie crumbs and worm candy in the cookie jar," Jessie said.

"Who would have been able to do that?" Henry asked.

"I don't know," Annika brushed her hair off her face. More of it had fallen out of the bun. "We always have treats out here after the tours. I set everything up early so I don't have to rush around when we get back. I don't know who would have come into the backyard."

"Sometimes people play tricks around Halloween," Violet said. "Maybe that's all it is."

"I don't know," Henry said. "This kind of trick would take a lot of effort. It's a really mean, scary trick. Why would anyone do that to Annika?"

A ghostly voice came from the path. "I'm coming to haunt you!"

Benny grabbed Jessie's hand. "Who...who said that?"

CHAPTER 3

The First Clue

"Isiah, stop with the voices," Annika called. She sounded angry.

A very tall and skinny young man came around the side of the house. He wore a black suit with a ruffled shirt and a tall black hat.

When he saw the Aldens and Mrs. McGregor, he swept his hat off his head and bowed. "Isiah Sanders at your service."

Violet whispered to Benny. "He looks like a character from a book."

"Where have you been?" Annika asked.

"You were supposed to drive the wagon!"

"You're mad at me, aren't you?" Isiah dropped down to his knees in front of her and clasped his hands in front of him. "Please forgive me," he begged. "I can't go on unless you do." He looked over at the Aldens and winked.

The children laughed at the performance.

"Oh, get up, Isiah," Annika said. "Now is not the time for acting."

He did, brushing the dirt off his knees. "I'm sorry I missed the tour. The harness on the wagon broke, and I lost my phone. I was coming to meet you with my car when the tire went flat. Why is it so dark? And where is the tour group?"

Henry thought Annika's friend was making a lot of excuses. It was hard to believe that so many bad things could happen to one person in such a short time.

Annika explained, "We heard some spooky noises in the woods on the first part of the tour. It sounded like there was something or someone out there following us. The tour guests weren't happy at all. And then you weren't there with the wagon."

"Are you sure the sounds you heard in the woods weren't just from an animal?" Henry asked.

"It sounded like a very big animal, even bigger than a deer," Annika said. "And deer don't make that much noise."

"That's a mean trick for someone to play," Isiah said.

"It was. I wish you had been there. You have to be more careful with your phone," Annika scolded. "I need someone I can count on to help me with the tours."

"Let me make it up to you. I'll lead the next tour and you take the easy job and drive the wagon. You know I'm good at telling stories and doing voices." He hunched over and then spoke in creaky, trembly voice like an old man. "I'll have them quivering in their boots. He pointed at Benny with a crooked finger. "Young man, you there? I see a strange, ghostly shape. Right behind you!" he yelled. Benny jumped, twisting around to look.

Benny's eyes opened wide and then he smiled. "I knew there wasn't really anyone there. I'm not that easy to trick."

"Just teasing you, young lad." Isiah laughed. "See, I'm good, aren't I?"

Annika stomped her foot and scowled at him. "This is supposed to be a family-friendly ghost tour, Isiah. Remember? We don't want them quivering in their boots."

"The tour has to be a little bit scary or else no one will want to go," Isiah said. "Can I have a cookie?" He reached for the cookie jar and then stopped. Jessie noticed a funny expression cross Isiah's face. "Come to think of it," Isiah said. "I'd rather have a cruller. I'm hungry."

Annika sighed. "You're the only person I know who is always hungry."

"You know two people now!" Benny said. "I'm always hungry too."

"There, you see," Isiah said, holding up his hand to high-five Benny. "Some people just need to eat. I should be going. I promise I'll be there tomorrow." He said good-bye to everyone.

After he left, Annika slumped down on one of the benches. "I guess the ghost-tour business was a bad idea. Maybe I should just quit."

"No, it's too soon to give up," Mrs. Vanderhoff told her.

"Can we go with you tomorrow?" Henry asked. "We might be able to help find out who is playing tricks."

"That's a good idea," Mrs. McGregor said. "If anyone can help solve this mystery, it's these four."

"You can come," Annika said. "But I don't think it will help."

"Annika, you sound very tired." Mrs. Vanderhoff said. "Things will seem better in the morning." She got up. "Why don't we all go to bed?"

She took the Aldens up to the apartment and showed them the sleeping bags on the floor. "I set everything up for you before it got dark. There are flashlights for each of you on the table and extra blankets on the sofa. Are you sure you'll be all right?"

"We'll be fine," Jessie said.

"Good night, then." After she left, Watch inspected each sleeping bag. He picked a dark green one and then lay down on it, closing his eyes.

"Watch is tired too," Violet said. "Someone is going to have to share their bed with him."

"I will," Benny said. "He can watch out for me. Watch can watch me, get it?"

"That's good, Benny," Violet said. "Let's all go to bed. I'm as tired as Watch."

Once they were all in their pajamas, Benny asked, "That wasn't really a headless horseman, was it?"

"No, it was someone dressed up like that," Jessie said. "There's an old story about a headless horseman by an author named Washington Irving. It's set in Sleepy Hollow. We read it in school."

"I don't know why someone would want to dress up like that," Benny grumbled. "It's too scary."

"We'll find out who did it and then you'll see it's just a trick," Henry said.

***

They woke the next morning when Mrs. McGregor came in the door. She had a tray with mugs of hot chocolate. "Good morning! The power is still out, but as soon as you're dressed, we're going next door to the restaurant for breakfast. I hear they have very tasty apple pancakes."

Benny jumped up. "Let's go!"

"Not in pajamas!" Jessie said, laughing.

"Oh, right," Benny said, looking down at his pajamas. "I forgot."

Mrs. McGregor picked up Watch's leash. "I'll take Watch and give him his breakfast," she said. "He can stay in the backyard while we go to the café. Come along, Watch."

When the Aldens were ready, they walked over to the café with Mrs. Vanderhoff and Mrs. McGregor. "Annika won't be joining us," Mrs. Vanderhoff said. "I'm afraid she has a bad headache. She is still upset about last night."

"I'd be upset too," Jessie said.

"Yes, we don't like when people play mean tricks," Henry added.

In front of the café a man wearing a jacket and a tie was watching two workers attaching a sign to a post outside the restaurant. The sign had a big red apple on it.

"I can read the sign!" Benny said. "It's called the Apple House Café!"

"Good job, Benny," Jessie said. "You're learning fast."

"Good morning, Mr. Beekman," Mrs. Vanderhoff said. "What a nice new sign."

The man mumbled something and then turned away from them.

Mrs. Vanderhoff shook her head sadly at the man's reaction and said, "Let's go on in."

As they walked up the steps, one of the workmen said, "This paint isn't dry! It's all over my hands. We shouldn't be putting up this sign now."

"I want it done today," Mr. Beekman said. "Put it up and I'll repaint it if it needs it."

He added something else, but the Aldens couldn't hear because a hostess opened the door of the café and said, "Welcome to the Apple House Café." She showed them to a big round table in the back and gave them menus.

A few minutes later a waiter in a red apron appeared. He scowled at them. Violet thought he looked a little like the man outside, but much younger. Both had curly brown hair and round faces.

"Good morning, Brett," Mrs. Vanderhoff said.

The young man didn't respond to her greeting as he pulled out an order pad. "We're busy," he snapped. "There's going to be a long wait for your food. What do you want?" He took down their orders for pancakes, eggs, bacon, coffee, and orange juice before hurrying away.

"The people who work here don't seem very friendly," Violet said.

"It's just Brett and his father," Mrs. Vanderhoff said. "I'm afraid they aren't very happy with me. They offered to buy my house at a good price. They want to turn it into a bed and breakfast for Brett to run. I just don't want to sell. I love my little shop, even if it doesn't make much money."

"Could Mr. Beekman be the one playing the tricks?" Henry asked. "He may think the tricks will convince you to sell the house."

"We know he has red paint," Violet said.

"And someone who owns a restaurant might know about food that looks like worms and dirt," Jessie added.

"Oh, I hope he wouldn't do that." Mrs. Vanderhoff looked shocked. "That wouldn't be very neighborly. I'm sure it's someone else."

Brett stomped over with a coffee pot and a pitcher of juice. He set the juice down with a thunk and some of it sloshed onto the tablecloth. "Oops," he said as he walked away.

The Aldens looked at each other. They weren't so sure.

CHAPTER 4

The Lost Scarecrow

A young woman came into the café and waved when she saw them.

"That's my other daughter Margot," Mrs. Vanderhoff said.

"She looks like Annika," Mrs. McGregor said. Margot had wavy blond hair like Annika but she looked a few years older.

When Margot sat down, Mrs. Vanderhoff introduced everyone and added, "Margot can tell you about Sleepy Hollow. She works for the county tourist office. She knows all about the history of the place and the wonderful things to see in the area."

"You've come to visit us at the right time," Margot said. "Halloween is the spookiest time of year in the spookiest town in America."

"Is Sleepy Hollow really the spookiest town?" Benny asked.

"It will be if I have my way," Margot said. "There's a contest going on in a travel magazine. I'm submitting an entry for our town. If we win, more tourists will visit us."

"How will the contest be judged?" Jessie asked. "Isn't it hard to prove a place is spooky?"

"I'll send in some of the pictures I've been taking of scary places and scary things around town. I'm also writing down all the unexplained hauntings we've had. The headless horseman from last night is a perfect story."

"Your sister was very upset by that," Mrs. Vanderhoff said.

"She shouldn't have been." Margot looked annoyed. "I don't think her ghost-tour business is going to work. It's silly to have a ghost tour that's not scary."

"You should support your sister's idea,"

Mrs. Vanderhoff said. "Annika is trying very hard to earn some money for the house repairs. We need a new roof."

"Mother, you should just sell the house to Mr. Beekman," Margot said. "You could use the money to rent a shop in a better location right downtown, and get yourself an apartment. Then you wouldn't have to worry about the roof. Plus, the town needs a gift shop on the main street."

"I love our house. It's been in our family too long to sell it because it requires some work." She poured herself some coffee. "Would you please pass me the sugar, Violet?"

Violet handed the bowl and its tongs to Mrs. Vanderhoff. Benny watched with interest as Mrs. Vanderhoff used the tongs to take a sugar cube out of the sugar bowl. She dropped it into her coffee.

"I didn't know sugar came in little blocks like that," Benny said. "Can I try one?"

"Just one," Jessie said. "Too much sugar isn't good for you."

He popped on in his mouth. "This is a good treat!"

Just then Brett brought their breakfasts. "Pancakes will be a better treat," Jessie said. She handed the syrup to Benny.

He poured the syrup on his pancakes and then took a big bite of one. "Even if the people aren't nice here, they make good pancakes."

Mrs. Vanderhoff smiled. "I'm glad you like them. Maybe after breakfast you children would like to make a scarecrow. There's a scarecrow contest at the library this afternoon. Annika made one, and we have all the supplies to build another.

"That would be so much fun!" Violet said.

"I'll be there taking pictures," Margot said. "There are always some amazing scarecrows in the contest."

Mrs. Vanderhoff turned to Henry. "We have wood for you to make a frame for the scarecrow. While you're doing that, your brother and sisters can look in the attic for old clothes to dress it up."

"Do we have to make a scary scarecrow?" Benny asked. "I'm not sure I want to do that."

"No, you can make any kind of scarecrow you like," Mrs. Vanderhoff said.

When they were finished with breakfast, she took them over to the house and up to the attic. "Use anything you want. The old trunks are full of clothes. If you need anything, just come downstairs and ask."

"I'll go make the frame," Henry said. "When you find something to put on the scarecrow you can bring it out to the garage. We can stuff it full of straw out there."

Jessie opened one of the trunks. "Should we make a girl scarecrow? There are some good dresses here."

"How about a lady in purple?" Violet suggested, picking up a long purple dress.

"Okay," Benny agreed. "That's not scary."

"Here's a good hat for her." Jessie said. She pulled out a big straw hat with a pink bow on it.

The three of them went to find Henry. He had already finished the frame and was putting away the tools while Watch followed him around. The children took the frame out into the yard, dressed the scarecrow, and stuffed it with straw.

When they were finished, Watch came over and growled at it.

"Watch doesn't like scarecrows," Violet said.

"It's because it doesn't have a head," Benny said. "I don't like headless scarecrows either. How do we fix it?"

"We could stuff a paper bag to use as the head," Jessie suggested. She went inside to ask Mrs. Vanderhoff for one and returned with a large grocery bag.

"Now it needs a face," Henry said.

Violet said, "I'll get my art supplies." She

brought down her markers and drew a lady's face onto the paper bag. When she was done, Henry attached the head to the scarecrow. Jessie put the hat on it. They stood back to look.

"It doesn't look quite right," Henry said. "But I don't know why."

Jessie laughed. "We forgot something important! It's missing hair!"

"How can we make hair?" Benny asked. "Bald scarecrows are almost as scary as headless ones."

"Maybe Mrs. Vanderhoff has some yarn," Violet suggested.

Mrs. Vanderhoff had yarn in shades of green, pink, and orange. "Let's use pink," Violet said. "That goes with the bow on the hat."

When they were done, they carried it around to the front of the house and onto the porch. Mrs. Vanderhoff and Mrs. McGregor came outside.

"What a wonderful scarecrow!" Mrs. Vanderhoff exclaimed. "It will stand out in the crowd."

The Aldens spent the rest of the morning helping Mrs. Vanderhoff in the shop. Jessie dusted while Benny and Violet made black and orange paper chains to decorate the front windows. Henry fixed a loose hinge on the door to the storeroom. Annika came downstairs when she felt better and helped too.

After lunch, Henry and Jessie loaded the scarecrow into Annika's car. She drove them downtown to the library. The lawn in front was filled with rows and rows of colorful scarecrows.

"Look at that one with the big red nose!" Benny said. "It's a clown scarecrow. I see one that looks like a cowboy. I'm glad there are scarecrows that aren't scary."

"Is there room for ours?" Violet asked.

"We'll ask Isiah," Annika said. "He works at the library and is organizing the contest this year."

"Is that him?" Benny pointed at a man wearing a wizard costume with a long white beard.

"Yes, he loves any excuse to dress up,"

Annika said. "He wants to be a professional actor some day."

Isiah saw them coming and hurried over to meet them. "What a great scarecrow," he said. "Or maybe we should call it a scare lady. Would you like to dance, miss?" He took the scarecrow from Henry and twirled it around.

Everyone laughed.

When he stopped, Jessie asked, "Where can we put it?"

Isiah handed the scarecrow back to Henry. "I've put plenty of poles, so let's find one that isn't claimed yet."

They found a spot in one of the back rows and set up the scarecrow. When they were finished, they went to look at the other contestants.

"There's Margot taking pictures," Jessie pointed.

Margot looked up and waved at them.

Loud voices made them turn toward the street. A group of young men piled out of a car, laughing and joking with one another. "There's Brett Beekman from the restaurant," Violet said, motioning to one of them.

The four young men ambled up to the scarecrows. One of them laughed and pointed at a scarecrow in an old ripped dress. "That looks like the old lady who works in the library," he said.

"It looks better than the old lady," another one said.

They all laughed and then Brett yelled, "There's Margot! Margot, take a picture of us! We're more interesting than scarecrows."

She rolled her eyes and ignored them.

"They're rude, aren't they?" Benny said to Violet. Violet nodded her head.

Brett and his friends drew closer. Brett pulled a witch scarecrow off its stake. "Who's scared of witches? She's going to get you." He swung it close to Violet and Benny and said, "Better run, kiddies, before the witch turns you into a couple of toads." Jerking it toward them, he yelled, "Boo!"

Benny jumped and cried out, "Stop!"

Brett's friends laughed again. Jessie crossed her arms in front of her and frowned. "Stop that. You're scaring my little brother."

"I'm just teasing," Brett said.

"It's mean teasing," Henry said.

Isiah rushed over to them. "Put that scarecrow back!" he ordered Brett. When Brett didn't move, Isiah grabbed it from his hands. "What are you doing here? This doesn't seem like your kind of fun."

"We can go wherever we want." Brett stared at Isiah's costume. "Why don't you dress in normal clothes? You look like a freak."

Isiah looked angry. "I've got a job to do, a real job, not one my father got for me."

Brett clenched his fists and took a step toward Isiah.

"Stop, you two," Annika said. "Brett, why don't you leave Isiah alone? You've been mean to him for years. Don't you get tired of it?"

"I'm just joking around," Brett said. "He's the one who can't take a joke." He walked away to join his friends.

"Let's forget about him," Jessie said. "Annika, where is your scarecrow?"

"I don't know where Isiah put it," Annika said. "But it should be easy to find. It looks just like the one in front of the shop."

"It's in the second row on the end," Isiah said. He put the witch scarecrow back on the pole. "I'll show you."

They followed after him to the end of the row, but the pole was empty. There was no headless scarecrow in a black cape. "That's strange," Isiah said. "I know it was here yesterday afternoon."

"Maybe someone moved it," Benny said.

"We'll look for it," said Jessie.

"Let's split up," Henry suggested.

A few minutes later, Jessie motioned for the rest to join her. "I found it," she said. "It's under a pine tree on the side of the library."

"Why would anyone move it there?" Annika asked.

Jessie didn't answer the question. "You should come look," she said in a low voice, her eyes darting around the crowd, "but I don't think we should let anyone else see it. It's bad."

CHAPTER 5

Beware

Henry, Violet, and Benny followed Jessie.

As they drew closer, Violet asked, "Why is the straw scattered everywhere?"

"Someone took out all the straw!" Benny said.

"That's not the worst." Jessie pointed at the pumpkin head. It had been smashed, and spattered with the same fake blood. It lay in pieces scattered around the scarecrow's body.

"What's that?" Benny asked, pointing a

trembling finger at a piece of paper on the scarecrow's chest.

Henry knelt down. "It's a note." He pulled it free and held it up. The word *BEWARE* was scrawled on it in the same color as the spattered red.

"That's horrible," Violet shuddered.

"Even if it's just a scarecrow, it's a bad thing to do," Benny said.

"What's going on back here?" Margot's voice came from behind them.

"Someone ruined my scarecrow," Annika told her sister.

Margot smiled when she saw the scarecrow on the ground. "Wow! What a great picture this will make." She snapped several pictures.

"Margot! Is that all you can think of?" Annika cried. "Someone did this on purpose."

"I can use it in the 'Most Haunted Town in America' entry. Can you children move out of the way so I can get a better shot?" Margot took more photos, which attracted the attention of the people admiring the scarecrows in the contest. Soon, a crowd of people was gathered around the damaged scarecrow.

"Annika, isn't that your ghost-tour scarecrow?" a woman asked.

Annika nodded. "Yes. I don't know who would do this."

"Why does it say *BEWARE*?" a boy asked. "Does it mean beware of the ghost tour?"

"No," Annika said. "I think it's just someone playing a joke. My ghost tours are fun and not scary."

"That's not what I've heard," the woman said. "I heard the last one frightened several children." Annika tried to explain but the woman wouldn't listen. "We won't be going on it," she said as she walked away.

The Aldens helped Annika pick up the pieces of her scarecrow. They could tell she was discouraged.

"Don't worry, Annika," Jessie said. "We're determined to find out who is playing these tricks."

"Who could have had a chance to move the scarecrow?" Henry asked.

"Anyone," Annika's face was glum. "I helped Isiah put it up yesterday. Someone could have moved it in the night. Let's go home."

Back at the house, the Aldens raked leaves for Mrs. Vanderhoff. When they were finished, Jessie got a notebook out of her suitcase. "Let's write down what we know about these terrible tricks and who could have done them," she said.

"Even though Mrs. Vanderhoff thinks Mr. Beekman wouldn't play the tricks, we should add him to the list," Henry said.

"And Brett too," Violet added. "He is very rude and mean."

"We should add the headless horseman to the list," Benny said.

"Benny, you know there's no real headless horseman," Jessie told him. "It's just a story."

"We've seen a headless horseman," Benny insisted. "He needs to be on the list."

"All right, I'll add him, but we need to think of other possibilities." Jessie wrote *headless horseman* in her notebook.

"What about Margot?" Henry asked. "She wants to get the town named the spookiest in America. She knows all about how Annika does the tours. She could have put the cookie crumbs and the candy worms in the cookie jar."

"But Margot is Annika's sister!" Violet shook her head. "That would be too mean."

"Maybe Margot doesn't realize it is mean," Henry said. "She might think it will help Annika's business if the town is named the spookiest."

"When Margot saw Annika's scarecrow, she didn't seem to notice that Annika was upset," Jessie added. "Mrs. Vanderhoff said Margot should have been at home last night when Annika called. Since she wasn't there, *she* could have ridden the horse. I'll write her name down too."

Mrs. Vanderhoff called them for dinner before they could think of more names. They ate quickly so they would be ready for the ghost tour. After dinner, Mrs. McGregor said, "I'll feed Watch and put him up in the apartment until you get back. Mrs. Vanderhoff and I are going to visit some of her friends, so we might not be back until after you are home."

"Poor Watch. I'm sorry you have to stay home," Benny said.

"Don't worry about Watch," Mrs. McGregor said. "He's been chasing squirrels all afternoon in the backyard. I'm sure he's very tired."

When everyone had their coats on, they walked with Annika to the tour's meeting point. A group of eight people arrived for the tour, four adults and four children, two girls and two boys. The boys were twins. One of the little girls announced, "I'm the birthday girl. I'm five."

"I'm five too," the twins said together.

The other girl said, "I'm almost five. I think." She looked up at her mother.

"Almost," her mother said. "In a year." Everyone laughed.

Annika wore her cape and carried a lantern with a candle in it. "I have a box of battery powered lanterns too," she said. "Anyone who might feel scared can carry one of these. I want you to have fun." All the younger children asked for lanterns, including Benny and Violet.

As they walked into the woods, Annika told them stories from the town's history. "People used to think there was a witch who lived in the forest," she said. "But she turned out to be something very different." Before she could finish the story, a loud cracking noise came from the trees on the side of the path. The group stopped.

"I think I saw something in the trees," one of the twins said. "Something big."

"Sometimes it's easy to imagine you see something when it's just the trees," Jessie told him. "It could be just a clump of bushes."

"Jessie is right," Annika said. "Let's keep going." She smiled, but the Aldens knew she was worried. They walked on, though everyone seemed a little nervous. Annika started her story again when another cracking noise came from behind them.

A sudden shriek startled them all. Everyone spun around, trying to see what had made the awful noise.

"That might have been an animal," Henry said.

Far down the path, a large, dark shape burst out of the woods. It made a loud snorting sound.

Everyone all stood very still.

Two red circles of light appeared, glowing in the dark.

"Are those eyes?" Violet whispered.

"I think so," Benny said. "But what has red eyes?"

"If those are eyes, that thing would have to be about ten feet tall," Henry said.

The lights disappeared, but the shape moved toward them. It came slowly at first and then faster and faster. It shrieked again.

"We should get off the path," Jessie yelled.

They all rushed into the woods just as the creature thundered past them. They could see it was a horse with a rider who wore a cape. In the light of Annika's lantern, they could see that the rider didn't seem to have a head.

The youngest girl in the group screamed and ran to her mother. One of the twins burst into tears. The parents of the twins each rushed to pick up one of the little boys.

"Pick me up too, Daddy!" the older girl said as she held up her arms to him.

"Please calm down," Annika said. "I'm sorry, but that was someone playing a trick." She sounded like she was going to cry too.

"We know that was just a horse," Henry

said, stepping back out onto the path. "Horses don't have glowing red eyes. We should see if we can find any clues about who is playing these tricks." He started to jog toward where the horse and its rider had first appeared on the path.

"Henry, I can't let you do that," Annika called after him.

"I'll just be a minute," Henry replied over his shoulder

"No!" Annika yelled. She ran after him and grabbed his sleeve when she caught up. "I'm responsible for you. Let's just stay calm and meet Isiah. The wagon will be waiting for us."

Henry could tell she was very upset. "All right, but I'm sure there is nothing dangerous back there."

Violet turned and looked in the other direction. "I hope Isiah is okay," she said. "The horse and rider will be riding right past where he's waiting with the wagon."

Annika tried to smile at the parents and children. "I'm...I'm sure he's fine. Jessie, would you and Benny walk with the group while Violet and Henry and I go ahead to make sure Isiah is...is ready for us?"

Jessie nodded. She was frightened but she knew Annika wanted her to be brave.

Henry and Violet followed Annika down the path, scared at what they might find. When they came to the wagon, they didn't see Isiah.

"What if the headless rider got him?" Violet asked.

Annika called out, "Isiah, where are you?"

CHAPTER 6

Costumes and More Clues

"I'm right here," Isiah called, sounding out of breath. He came around from the front of the wagon. "I was adjusting Ghost's harness."

"Did you see the horse run by?" Henry asked.

"What horse?" Isiah looked very puzzled.

"A big black horse chased us off the path!" Violet said. "It would have dashed right past you. It was making a horrible noise too."

"I didn't see anything," Isiah said. "I didn't hear anything either. I always listen to music while I'm waiting." He patted his coat pocket. "I keep my MP3 player and my earbuds with me. Though the horses were both restless for some reason."

Henry thought Isiah sounded like he was telling the truth, but Henry couldn't figure out what had happened to the horse. He supposed it might have gone off the path into the woods, just like it had appeared onto the path.

Jessie, Benny, and the rest of the group arrived. The children were no longer crying, but none of them were smiling.

Isiah bowed to the tour group and said, "Good evening. Ghost and Spook and I welcome you." He motioned to the two white horses hitched to a big open wagon. No one said anything. He held his lantern up and looked around at the group. "Looks like we have a quiet crowd tonight. No one is laughing. Shall I tell you a funny story?"

"No," Annika said. "We should just go back to the shop." She helped the smaller children into the wagon.

"Isiah, did you fall down?" Benny asked.

"You have mud on your face and your coat is ripped."

Annika turned and examined Isiah. "Benny is right. What happened?"

Isiah rubbed his muddy cheek. "Benny guessed it. I'm just clumsy. When I got out of the wagon to tighten the harness, I slipped in the mud."

Jessie started to speak and then stopped. It hadn't rained since they had been in Sleepy Hollow, and she didn't see any mud. She would note it in her notebook when she got back to the Vanderhoffs.

On the way back, Annika tried to teach the tour group an old folk song. The Aldens joined in but the other children were still fearful. They held up their lanterns and looked out into the darkness. Jessie could hear the parents grumbling to each other about the scare they'd had. When the tour arrived back to the house, the group didn't want to stay for the treats and asked for their money back. Annika gave it to them, apologizing.

When the tour group was gone, Isiah

said, "Now are you going to tell me what happened?"

Annika started to cry, so Henry explained what had happened.

"Not another trick," Isiah groaned.

"We were worried the horseman would get you," Violet said.

"Annika, you should really let me do the tours," Isiah said. "Look how upset you are."

"No, I can do them." Annika wiped her face. "I'm not going to let someone scare me with silly tricks."

"All right, but think about it." Isiah patted his horses. "I should get these old boys back to the stable. It's getting late."

After Isiah left, the Aldens helped Annika put away the treats and drinks. They were nearly finished when Violet said, "I hear a noise. I think someone is in the yard behind Mr. Beekman's café."

Henry walked to the fence. "Hello!" he called out, shining the flashlight.

"What do you want?" a man said in an angry voice. "Don't shine that light in my eyes."

"It's Mr. Beekman," Annika said. She

went over to the fence. "Good evening, Mr. Beekman. We were just worried when we heard a noise."

"Well, I'm allowed to go into my café whenever I want. I came to get something I'd forgotten."

"Sorry we bothered you," Henry said.

When they had finished cleaning up, Annika said, "Thank you for helping. I'm very tired, and I need to think about what to do about the tours. Good night."

The Aldens went up to the apartment. Henry looked out the window. "Mr. Beekman is leaving. He said he came to get something, but he's not carrying anything."

"Maybe it's something small, like a piece of paper he put in his pocket," Violet suggested.

"We have to figure this out," Henry said. "Annika was very upset tonight. If it happens again, she might stop her ghost tours."

Jessie told them about the lack of mud around the wagon. "I'm adding Isiah to the list," she said.

"We do know he likes to dress up in costumes," Violet said thoughtfully. "He likes to act too. Whoever is playing the tricks is good at pretending to be the headless horseman."

"Why would he play a trick on Annika?" Benny asked. "They are supposed to be friends. I like Isiah."

"I do too." Jessie took her notebook out but didn't write anything down.

"He really wants to be the one who does the ghost tours." Henry said, turning away from the window. "Maybe he's hoping she'll be so scared that she'll let him lead the tours."

"If Isiah had been riding a black horse, where did he put it?" Jessie asked. "We know it wasn't Ghost or Spook. You can't make white horses look black."

"That's part of the mystery," Violet said.

Jessie wrote down Isiah's name, but the rest of the Aldens could tell she didn't like his name on the list.

***

The next morning Jessie and the other children helped Mrs. Vanderhoff make more crullers.

"There are many different kinds of crullers, but I think my family's recipe is the best," Mrs. Vanderhoff said as they mixed the flour and cinnamon and other ingredients. "The shape is important. First, you take a piece of dough and roll it between your hands until it looks like piece of rope." She gave each of the Aldens their own dough to work with. Jessie did hers and then helped Benny.

When everyone had the dough in the right shape, Mrs. Vanderhoff showed them how to fold each piece in two so the dough looked like a braid. "Next we cut them into sections and fry them in hot oil. Be careful because the oil can spatter." She showed Jessie how to use tongs to put the dough in the oil. "When the doughnuts are nice and brown, we take them out and roll them in sugar."

"The most important part!" Benny said.

"I think the most important part is to taste them!" Henry teased.

While they were eating the crullers, Mrs. Vanderhoff said, "I want you all to enjoy yourselves while you're in town. Annika, why don't you take our guests to the Harvest Festival and the Halloween costume parade in the town square? There will be food booths and music and games. If you'd like to dress up in costumes, you might be able to find something in the attic to wear."

"We would like that," Jessie said. "There are some wonderful old clothes up there."

"I'll help you look for something," Annika said. "I might wear a costume too."

They hurried up to the attic, excited about the parade. "I feel bad that we have to leave Watch shut up while we're out having fun," Benny said.

"Watch can go too," Annika said as she opened one of the trunks. "Some people bring their dogs dressed up in costumes."

One trunk was full of colorful dresses covered in rows of fringe. There were headbands that matched, and each one had a big feather attached. "I think girls from the 1920s wore these sorts of dresses," Jessie said.

"That's right," Annika said. She put a blue headband on. "The girls who wore these dresses were called flappers."

"Flappers? That's funny," Benny said. "Did they do this?" He ran in a circle flapping his arms. Everyone laughed.

"Not like that," Jessie said, "but I want to be a flapper."

"Me too." Violet picked up a purple dress. "I'd like to wear this one." The dresses were too long for Jessie and Violet, so Mrs. McGregor helped them pin them up to the right length.

"This looks like a uniform." Henry put on a black jacket with gold stripes on the sleeves.

"That belonged to my grandfather," Annika said. "He was a pilot during World War II."

"Can I be a pilot too?" Benny asked.

Violet said, "I don't think there is another uniform. Even if there was, I'm afraid it wouldn't fit you."

Jessie picked up a battered brown hat. "You could wear this and be an explorer. I saw a man's brown shirt that matches. If we roll up the sleeves, you can wear that too."

"That's a good idea," Henry said. "I found an old metal water canteen. You could use that as part of the costume."

Once Benny had his costume together,

Violet said, "Now that we all have costumes, what is Watch going to wear?"

"How about this bow tie and vest?" Jessie said. "He can be a dog professor."

When they were ready, they went downstairs to the shop. Mrs. McGregor clapped her hands at the sight of them. "You look wonderful! Let me take a picture to show your grandfather."

Downtown, they found crowds of people. "I smell something good," Benny said as they walked through the festival.

"The Apple House Café has a booth here," Annika told him. "You're smelling their apple custard tarts. They're famous for that."

"I'd like to try one," Benny said, "but only if Brett and Mr. Beekman aren't there. I don't like mean people."

"I don't see them." Violet stood on tiptoes so she could see over the crowd. "Some other people are working there."

Everyone tried the tarts.

"These are delicious." Jessie nibbled on hers slowly, tasting each bite. "I want to learn to make these too."

"Mr. Beekman is too mean to give you the recipe," Annika said. "I'll ask my mother if she knows how to make them. We should go say hello to Isiah. He's working in the library booth."

"That booth that says *library*," Benny said. "I see a girl dressed as an elf, but not Isiah."

Annika greeted the girl and asked, "Isn't Isiah supposed to be working?"

The girl slammed down a box of bookmarks. "Yes, but he didn't show up. I can't believe he didn't even call."

"He's been doing that too often," Annika said. "If I see him, I'll remind him he's supposed to be working. We should go. It's almost time for the parade."

"Look at those funny costumes." Benny pointed to some adults dressed as zoo animals walking by the booth. They were all carrying musical instruments.

"That's the band that leads the parade," Annika said. "We can follow them to the starting point. I wonder where Margot is. I thought she'd be here taking pictures."

All the children and pets participating in the

parade gathered at one end of the street. The band struck up a tune. The children began to march as the bystanders clapped for them.

They were halfway down the block when Violet stopped. "There's the headless horseman." She pointed up the street where a figure wearing a big black cape sat on a large black horse. It looked like there was no head above the cape.

"Maybe it's part of the parade," Henry suggested. "They could have someone dress up in costume to make the end of the parade more exciting."

"There's something strange about the horse," Jessie said. "It has red all around its eyes and mouth. And the coat is too shimmery for a normal horse."

Other children around them began to point as the horse and rider came closer. "That horse is scary," a little girl dressed as a fairy said.

Watch growled.

The horse reared up and gave an angry neigh.

CHAPTER 7

The Horseman Strikes Again

The musicians in front slowed down, and the music trailed off. The children behind them slowed too.

"I don't think that person is part of the event," Violet said.

The horse began to move toward them, slowly at first, just like on the ghost tour.

"I don't like this," Benny said.

The rider kicked the horse's sides until it broke into a run, charging right at them.

"Get out of the way!" Jessie gasped. Most

of the children and the musicians scattered off the street. But Jessie noticed that two smaller children weren't moving. They were too confused.

Jessie picked up the girl in the fairy costume and carried her to safety. Henry took hold of the little boy in a superhero costume. He led him to the sidewalk just as the rider drew close. The rider pulled the horse to a stop, reached under the cape and took out a white pumpkin.

The father of the little boy ran up and grabbed his son, taking him away into the crowd. Jessie looked around for a parent to claim the little girl she held in her arms. She heard a woman yelling, "Samantha! Where are you!"

"Mommy, I'm here," the girl cried.

Before Jessie could find the woman, Violet said, "Uh-oh. I know what's going to happen."

The horseman raised the pumpkin up and then tossed it toward them. The pumpkin hit the ground right in front of Jessie and Violet. It split open, and dark red liquid spattered out. The rider kicked the horse again rode away down a side street.

The girl Jessie held screamed and began to cry. Her mother came up and took her from Jessie. "It's okay," the woman told the girl, but she was crying too. "Thank you!" she said to Jessie.

A boy in a fireman costume held out his hand. "I'm bleeding!"

"No," Benny said. "It's just paint. See?" Benny took his finger and wiped off a speck of paint from the boy's hand.

"Are you all right?" Annika called as she hurried over to them. She looked over her shoulder and turned back to the Aldens. "The mayor doesn't look happy."

Henry turned to see a big man in a dark suit stomping across the street toward them.

The man stopped in front of Annika. "How could you arrange a trick like that?" he asked. "That is not the way to get business for your tours. Look how you've frightened the children with your stunts."

"It wasn't me," Annika protested. "I don't know who was riding that horse."

"You expect anyone to believe that?" The mayor shook his finger at her. "I don't want anything like this happening again. If it does, the town council might not let you use your wagon after all." He turned and walked away.

Annika called after him. "It really wasn't me!"

The mayor didn't respond.

"What did he mean about the wagon?" Jessie asked.

"I had to get special permission from the town council to use it in the woods. If the council changes their mind, I'll have to change the whole tour. The wagon ride is one of the best parts of it. I don't know what to do."

"We have to find out who is playing these tricks and make them stop," Jessie said.

"Let's see if we can find any clues," Henry suggested. "I wish we had thought to run after the horse to see where they went."

"I don't think you're going to find any clues," Annika said. "There won't be any footprints on the street to follow."

"You might be surprised," Benny said. "We're good at finding clues."

The four of them walked to where they

had first seen the horse. They searched up and down for anything that could be a clue. The street was empty.

They were ready to give up when Jessie cried, "I found something!" She brushed her finger across a lamppost. When she held it up, they could see it was covered with something black and glittering. "The horse must have brushed against the post, and this is what made it all shimmery."

Violet touched her sister's finger. "It's a little sticky, like glitter glue."

Benny pointed at something on the street a few feet away. "What's that? He darted forward and picked it up. "It's a sugar cube, like the ones we saw at the café."

"Why would anyone carry sugar cubes?" Violet asked.

"I don't know, but it's a clue," Henry said. "Let's go tell Annika."

Before they could tell her, Margot came rushing up. "I can't believe I missed all that! How exciting! I hope my boss got pictures of it."

"Margot, it was terrible," Annika said.

"The mayor thinks I arranged it. I told him I didn't, but I don't think he believes me."

"Oh, don't worry about the mayor." Margot smiled. "As soon as we win the contest, he'll be happy about anything that helps the town seem scary. He'll even thank you." She waved at someone in the crowd. "There's my boss. I'll see you later."

"I'm ready to go home," Annika said. "The festival is ruined for me."

Back at the Vanderhoffs', Jessie got her notebook again. "We can't take anyone off our list with this latest trick. Brett, Mr. Beekman, Margo, and Isiah were not at the parade when the horseman appeared. Any one of them could have been the rider."

"We aren't making much progress," Violet said.

"I think we should look for clues on the ghost walk," Henry suggested. "And we should go now when there is still daylight."

"Good idea," Jessie said. "There have to be more clues somewhere."

"We can bring Watch," Benny said. "He'd like a walk."

They found the starting point for the ghost tour and walked down the path into the woods. "It isn't scary during the daytime," Benny said. "How are we going to know where we first saw the horse and the rider?"

"We had been walking a while," Henry said. "I remember the path went around a bend a little ways before we saw the horseman."

They found the right spot and searched carefully but didn't find anything.

"I think there are too many leaves." Benny scuffed through some. "And too many people have been walking through here."

"I'm sorry we didn't find anything, but it is very pretty here," Violet said. "I'd like to come back and sketch this part of the path. Look at that big tree. I like how the branch hangs over the path." She pointed and then lowered her arm, frowning. "There's something up in that tree that doesn't belong there."

CHAPTER 8

Missing

"I don't see anything," Jessie said.

"It's right above the big branch." Violet walked under the tree and pointed. "That black thing."

"I see it." Henry went over to the tree trunk. "I think I can climb up there." He found enough handholds and footholds to get up in the tree, and finally he crawled along the branch over the path.

He stopped and held up a short black plastic tube. "This is interesting," he said.

"It's tied to the branch." He reached inside, and withdrew two red glowing circles like big scary eyes.

"How did you do that?" Benny asked.

"There are two holes cut in this pipe." Henry lowered it down so it hung over the path. "Inside is a red glow stick with an on off switch."

"So that's how someone made it look like the horse had big glowing eyes," Jessie said. "It wasn't on the horse at all. Someone reached up and took it down when they rode the horse under it."

"We can take it and show Annika," Benny said.

"Why don't we leave it here and keep watch to see who is using it," Henry suggested. "If someone tried to scare Annika's tour once, he or she will probably do it again."

"But that means we'd have to wait in the woods in the dark." Benny looked around at the trees. "I don't know if I want to do that."

"You wouldn't have to, Benny." Jessie hugged him. "You could go on the tour with Annika. Let's go tell her the plan."

They hurried back to the house and told Annika about the glow stick and explained their plan to find out who was using it.

"That's a terrible trick," she said. "I don't know who would go to that much trouble to scare my groups. I have some other bad news. The people who were supposed to go on the tour tonight canceled. They have small children and they said they heard it was too scary. I'll never earn enough money for a new roof now."

"What about tomorrow night? Are some people scheduled to go on the tour then?"

"There are," Annika said. "If they don't cancel."

"You're worrying too much," Mrs. Vanderhoff said. "We'll manage somehow. I don't want you to spend your time dwelling on these tricks. I want you to have fun too. Why don't you take our guests to see a play? A theater group in town has turned the *Legend of Sleepy Hollow* story into a play."

Annika was quiet for a moment and then said, "That's a good idea. You've all been trying so hard to help me that I feel bad your vacation hasn't been more fun. I'll call Isiah too. He'll want to go see the play now that the tour has been canceled."

They met Isiah in front of the theater. He wasn't dressed in a costume, but he was wearing an old-fashioned brown suit with a brown hat.

"I like your fedora," Violet told him. "Old hats are fun to wear."

"Thank you," Isiah said. "I've got a whole hat collection. I've also got tickets for all of us." He handed everyone one a ticket.

When they had gone inside and found their seats, Jessie looked around. She saw a familiar face.

"Isn't that Brett?" she asked Annika. "That man next to the stage wearing headphones?"

"Yes," Annika said. "When we were in high school, Brett and his friends did the sound and lighting for the school plays. I don't like Brett, but he was good at that work. I didn't know he was helping the theater group."

"Is this play going to be scary?" Benny asked.

"A little," Henry said. "It's just a play

though. The headless horseman scares a man named Ichabod Crane."

"Ichabod? That's a very funny name," Benny said.

"Ichabod is a good part. I should have been cast," Isiah said. "I tried out for the play, but I didn't get the part. I think Brett convinced the director the role should go to one of his friends."

The lights in the theater dimmed and the play started. Several times during the show, the spooky sounds and lights startled the audience. When a big dark shadow that looked like a headless horseman chased Ichabod Crane, Benny whispered to Jessie, "This is not just a little scary, it's very scary."

After the play was done and the lights came back on, Jessie said, "That was very good. I felt like I was right in the forest."

"I did too," Violet said. "Even though there wasn't a real horse, that shadow made me afraid."

Annika said, "I have to admit Brett and his friends did a good job with the sounds and lights."

"Don't tell him that," Isiah said. "It'll go to his head, and his head is big enough already."

"It looks like a normal size to me." Benny sounded puzzled.

Everyone else laughed. "Having a big head means someone thinks they are better than everyone else," Jessie explained.

They were putting on their coats when someone behind Isiah yelled "Boo!"

Everyone jumped.

It was Brett. He laughed and slapped Isiah on the shoulder. "Isiah, you are still as jumpy as ever. I remember how scared you used to be when the theater went dark. When you go home tonight, you should watch out. You never know what's waiting for you." He laughed again and turned away.

"Brett and his friends need to grow up," Jessie said.

"They do," Isiah agreed. "They used to think it was funny to turn off the lights in the theater when no one expected it. It wasn't funny to anyone else."

"Just ignore him," Annika said.

Outside the theater, the wind had picked

up. It blew the fallen leaves into swirling patterns. Rain began to fall.

"Annika, can you give me a ride?" Isiah asked. "My car broke down."

"Of course," she said.

"How did you get here?" Henry asked.

"I walked through the cemetery, but it wasn't dark and stormy then. I'd rather not go back that way."

They were almost at Annika's car when Isiah stopped and patted his pocket. "Oh no. My cell phone is missing. It must have fallen out of my pocket inside the theater. I'll have to go back and look for it. You go on."

"We can wait for you," Annika said.

"No, I don't know how long it will take me to find it. I'll just get a ride from someone else. I'll see you tomorrow." He went back inside.

"Not again," Annika said. She shook her head and said to the Aldens, "Let's hurry to the car. I don't want to get soaked."

The Aldens and Annika got back to the Vanderhoffs' just as it began the rain began to fall very hard.

The storm got worse as the Aldens were getting ready for bed.

As they lay there listening to the thunder and lightning, Jessie said, "I hope Isiah got a ride. I wouldn't want to be outside in this. Maybe we should have waited for him."

"I hope he at least found his phone," Henry said. "I've never known anyone who loses things so much or has so many things go wrong. Remember that first night when he had a flat tire and lost his cell phone then too?"

"He also said the wagon wheel broke," Jessie added. "Then the night the horse nearly ran us down on the ghost tour, Isiah said he fell down and that's how he got muddy." She told them how she noticed there wasn't any mud around the carriage that night.

"Is Isiah lying about some of the things he claims happened to him?" Benny asked.

"I don't know," Violet said, "but all those things are suspicious." She yawned. "Let's talk in the morning. I think I can fall asleep now."

***

The next morning the Aldens helped Mrs.

Vanderhoff in the shop while they were waiting for the ghost tour to start.

After lunch, Annika said, "I'd better call Isiah and make sure he knows we have a tour tonight." She dialed and listened for a few moments before hanging up. "He's not answering."

"Maybe he couldn't find his phone," Jessie suggested.

"Yes. Knowing Isiah, he could have lost it anywhere," Annika said. "I guess I should go to his apartment and tell him in person. Would you all like to come with me? I want to treat you to some ice cream for all your hard work."

"We'll always say yes ice cream," Benny said. The rest of the Aldens agreed.

Isiah lived in an apartment in a big old house overlooking the cemetery. Annika rang the bell and the landlady came to the door. Annika explained they were looking for Isiah.

"You can knock on his door," the landlady told them. "But I don't think he's there. I haven't seen him since yesterday afternoon. His car has been here all night, but he hasn't."

"That's strange," Annika said.

"There's something else that's odd," the landlady said. "I found one of his hats in the back of the yard by the cemetery this morning." She picked up a hat from a table next to the door. It was the brown fedora Isiah had worn the night before.

"You would think he'd notice his hat fell off," Violet said.

"Maybe he couldn't get a ride after all," Henry suggested. "He could have been hurrying through the cemetery to get home because of the rain. The wind was blowing very hard last night."

"I'll call the library," Annika said. She took out her phone and dialed. She asked the person on the other end a few questions and frowned when she hung up. "He's not supposed to work today. They haven't seen him. I hope he shows up later. I don't know how I'll do the tour without the wagon. I'll call his parents. They live in town." She made another phone call.

Henry, Jessie, Violet, and Benny exchanged glances. They could tell Annika was becoming concerned.

When she hung up, her face was pale. "No one has seen or heard from him. Isiah is missing."

CHAPTER 9

Mystery in the Woods

"Isiah's father says he'll turn up, but I'm worried," Annika said. "I have to cancel the tour now. I don't have anyone else to drive the wagon."

"I have an idea," Henry said. "If you drive the wagon to the pick-up spot and left it there with us, we could watch over it until you arrive."

"That would be a big help." Annika smiled. "The horses are very gentle and well-trained. They won't give you any problems.

When it was time, Annika drove the Aldens to the stable. It was a long white building on the edge of town. When they pulled up in front of it, Henry said, "The sign says Sanders Stables. Does it belong to Isiah?"

"No, it belongs to Isiah's father." Annika got out of the car. "He has several horses they use for tourist trail rides and wagon rides. That's how I'm able to borrow one of their wagons."

"Could this be where the mystery horse lives?" Jessie asked. "It has to have a stable close to town."

"If it's a real horse," Benny said, "and not an evil spirit horse."

"It's a real horse," Violet said. "I'm sure of it."

"There's no all-black horse at the stable," Annika assured them. "I would have recognized it. I've been riding horses here for years."

A tall older man who looked a little like Isiah was feeding the horses inside. "Hello, Mr. Sanders. These are my friends." Annika introduced everyone.

"Isiah still hasn't shown up," Mr. Sanders told them.

"We'll manage without him," Annika said. "I need to hitch up the horses a bit early and get the wagon in place. If you do see Isiah, will you tell him to come to the meeting place?"

Mr. Sanders said he would.

"How many horses do you have here, Mr. Sanders?" Henry asked.

"About twenty. Some are too old to do more than loaf around most of the time." He rubbed the nose of the brown horse he was feeding.

A black-and-white horse at the end of the stalls stuck his head over the wall and looked at them.

"That's a pretty horse," Violet said.

Mr. Sanders snorted. "I've never thought of Domino as pretty. He's always had a bad temper and he bites. The older he gets, the crankier he acts. Isiah is the only one he likes because Isiah gives him treats. Too bad he's not like Ghost and Spook. They are good horses. Now let's get that wagon ready."

Ghost and Spook stood patiently while

Annika and Mr. Sanders showed the Aldens how to fasten the harnesses.

"Henry, if you'd like to drive the wagon, I'll show you how," Annika said. "We take the back roads so there aren't many cars."

Henry took the reins and drove the wagon along the back roads of Sleepy Hollow to the right spot.

Annika and the Aldens got down and fastened the reins to a tree. Annika pulled something out of her pocket. "Ghost and Spook should be fine, but if they get restless, just feed them a few of these." She held out some sugar cubes. "Sugar isn't good for them, but Isiah says it's all right once in a while." Ghost whinnied at the sight of the treats. "He loves them," Annika said. "Do you know how to feed a horse a treat?"

"Yes," Jessie said. "You hold your hand out flat with the treat in your palm."

"That's right. You don't want a horse thinking your fingers are a snack. They might nibble on them. Now I have to get my car and go home and change. Are you sure you'll be okay?"

"We're sure," Henry assured her.

As Annika hurried off, she said over her shoulder, "Just call me with your cell phone if you need anything."

Jessie petted Ghost's nose. Her brothers and sister could tell she was thinking about something.

"What are you thinking about?" Violet asked.

"At least we know that horse at the parade was not a ghost horse," she replied. "That sugar cube Benny found was a treat for him. Spirit horses don't eat treats."

"You're right," Henry said. "We should check the tube. It's going to be dark soon."

They walked down the path. Fallen leaves crunched beneath their feet, but otherwise the woods were silent.

"It is colder than it was last night," Violet said, pulling her hat down on her head.

"It's getting dark faster than I thought it would," Henry said. "We should hurry."

A loud crack came from down the path, and then a groaning noise. The Aldens froze in place. They waited, but there were no other sounds.

"What do we do?" Violet whispered.

"We keep going," Henry said. "That sounded like a human groan, not a ghost groan."

They crept as quietly as they could down the path. "It's just around this bend," Jessie said.

They came to the big tree. "The tube is still there." Benny pointed out it.

"I see something is different." Henry walked over to the trunk. "That branch wasn't broken before. I used it to get up in the tree."

"Maybe a big animal crashed into it and broke it," Violet said.

Henry shook his head. "Look where it broke, along the top, just like when someone is climbing a tree and the branch won't hold them. When that happens, it breaks at the trunk first."

"So that means someone was climbing up the tree," Jessie said.

Benny fell to the ground. "And he fell down like this!"

"And then he groaned because it hurt,"

Violet added. "But whoever did it ran off. Let's see if we can find some clues to tell us which way he or she ran."

While they were looking, Henry's cell phone rang. Annika was calling. He put her on speaker so they could all hear. "Everyone has canceled their spots on the tour." She sounded very upset. "I'll be there soon to help bring the wagon back. We won't be able to find out who is playing the tricks tonight after all."

"I don't think anyone will try tonight." Henry explained about the broken branch. "We think whoever is playing tricks fell and got hurt."

"We may never solve this mystery," Annika said and sighed. "I'll be there soon."

When she arrived, they took the horses back to the stable and then drove to the Vanderhoffs'. Margot was outside by the fire with Mrs. Vanderhoff and Mrs. McGregor. She was very interested to hear the story of the broken branch and the tube. "Whoever is doing that is very clever," she said.

"It may be clever, but it's not very nice," Violet said.

Jessie went to get her notebook. She brought it back to the fire and sat down. "I've been thinking. Are there other stables around town where the mystery horse could live?"

Margot shuddered. "Don't ask me. I don't keep track of the horses in town."

"You don't like horses?" Violet asked.

"Not at all." Margot shuddered again. "They're so big that they could trample you if they got angry. I should be going. Busy day tomorrow. Let me know if you see or hear anything else that's scary."

After Margot left, Mrs. Vanderhoff explained, "Margot has been frightened of horses ever since she was a little girl. A horse stepped on her foot one time."

"So I guess that means she doesn't ride horses," Henry said.

Annika laughed. "She certainly doesn't. She wouldn't even ride a horse on a merry-go-round."

Benny yawned. "I'm getting sleepy. Ghost tours even without ghosts make me tired."

"It's time for bed." Jessie closed her

notebook. "We'll make a new plan in the morning."

When the Aldens were inside the apartment, Henry said, "At least we know Margot didn't play the tricks. If she's so scared of horses, she's not the rider."

"That leaves Isiah, Mr. Beekman, or Brett." Violet went to the window and looked out into the dark. "One of them is still out there planning more tricks."

CHAPTER 10

Help from a Horse

The next morning after breakfast, the Aldens helped Annika rake leaves and clean up outside the front of the shop. They saw Mr. Beekman struggling to carry a big box up the steps of the café. His ankle was wrapped in a bandage.

"Let me help you," Henry offered, hurrying to the café.

Mr. Beekman looked surprised, but said, "Thank you. I was afraid I was going to drop it."

Mrs. Vanderhoff came out of the shop. "Mr. Beekman, what happened to your ankle?" she asked.

"I sprained it when I tripped over a broken step in back," he said.

"You should get one of your workers to carry things in," Mrs. Vanderhoff scolded. "The ankle won't get better unless you rest it."

Mr. Beekman shook his head. "I can't. They're all busy with other jobs. We're having a special charity dinner tonight to raise money for the library."

"We can help," Jessie offered.

"Yes," Mrs. Vanderhoff added. "We'll all help. Just tell us what you want us to do."

Mr. Beekman frowned and asked, "Why would you help me?"

"I like to be neighborly," replied Mrs. Vanderhoff. "And I'm happy to do anything that helps the library."

Mr. Beekman took his volunteers to the backyard. Mrs. Vanderhoff and Mrs McGregor set the tables that had been placed there while Jessie, Henry, and Annika helped string paper lanterns around the trees. Violet and Benny did the centerpieces. Benny scattered colorful leaves on the table and Violet arranged miniature pumpkins and pinecones around small pots of yellow mums.

When they were done, Mr. Beekman said, "I can't thank you enough. I couldn't have done it without you." He turned to Mrs. Vanderhoff. "I want to apologize. Ever since you said you weren't selling your house, I haven't been very nice to you. I realize how unkind that is."

"Apology accepted." Mrs. Vanderhoff gave him a big smile.

"Why don't you all come in for a snack?" Mr. Beekman said.

Mrs. Vanderhoff and the Aldens followed him inside and sat down at a table. He brought them hot chocolate and a plate of his apple custard tarts.

"Hello!" Isiah called out from the front door of the café. He came over to their table and did a funny little dance like a jig. "It's a wonderful day. I have some wonderful news."

"Where have you been?" Annika asked.

Isiah pointed at himself. "You are looking at an actor who has a real part in a real play in New York City. I found out the other night. I took the train into the city right away so I could sign the contract."

"Congratulations!" Annika said. "But you could have told someone," she grumbled. "We've been worried."

"I couldn't find my cell phone, but I left you a note. I taped to the front door of the shop."

"We didn't see any note," Mrs. Vanderhoff said. "It must have blown away."

While Isiah was telling Annika about the play, Henry pulled the rest of the Aldens aside. "So now we know it wasn't Isiah and it wasn't Margot. That leaves Mr. Beekman or Brett."

"Mr. Beekman said he fell down the steps, but he could have sprained his ankle falling out of a tree," Jessie said.

"Brett is the meanest one though," Violet said. "I think it was him."

"How are we going to find out which one it is?" Benny asked as he reached over to take a sugar cube out of the bowl.

"Benny, your hot chocolate doesn't need anymore sugar!" Jessie said.

Henry took a sugar cube of his own. "This gives me an idea," he said. "Anyone else guess what I'm thinking? Benny isn't the only one who likes sugar cubes."

Violet nodded. "I bet I can guess what your idea is."

Henry got up and went over to Mr. Beekman. "Could you and Brett do us a big favor?"

"Of course," Mr. Beekman said. "You've helped me out. I'll help you out."

"We need you to come to Sanders Stable, just for a few minutes," Henry said. "I'll explain there."

Mr. Beekman looked very puzzled but agreed to go. He went to get Brett, who did not seem pleased at Henry's request.

When they all reached the stable, Isiah's father was outside washing out brushes.

"We just need to see the horses for few minutes," Jessie told him.

"I usually don't have folks come just to visit the horses, but you're welcome to come in." He showed them inside. Domino looked out of his stall and neighed at the sight of them. Mr. Sanders frowned. "I wonder what's gotten into him."

"Let's go see," Violet suggested.

They walked down to the end of the row of stalls. Henry motioned to the front of Domino's stall. "Mr. Beekman and Brett, would you just stand together right here?"

"I don't know why you want us to do that, but I guess you'll tell us soon enough," Mr. Beekman said.

The Beekmans moved into place.

Domino stuck his head out and butted it against Brett's chest, whinnying softly.

"I don't believe it," Mr. Sanders said. "I think he likes you."

"Why don't you give him a treat?" Henry said, taking some sugar cubes from his pocket. He tried to hand one to Brett, but Brett wouldn't take it.

Domino neighed, sounding angry.

"I think you should give the horse the treat," Mr. Sanders said. "When Domino gets angry, sometimes he kicks the stall door."

"Go ahead, Brett," Mr. Beekman said.

Brett fed Domino the sugar cube. The horse rubbed his nose against Brett's chest and whinnied again. "He acts like he knows you," Mr. Sanders said.

Brett didn't say anything but he looked uncomfortable.

"Mr. Sanders, could we see where you keep the grooming supplies?" Jessie asked.

"They're in the tack room." He opened the door to a small room across from Domino's stall. "The brushes are drying outside, but most of the other supplies are in that cabinet."

"May I look in the cabinet?" Violet asked.

Mr. Sanders nodded. Violet opened it and examined the containers and jars. She reached in and took out a jar full of black glittery gel.

Mr. Sanders took a step back in surprise. "I don't know how that got in there. People use that on horses in parades and horse shows. We don't have any need for that here."

Violet pulled out two cans. "These say horse paint. There is one can of black and one can of red."

"Isiah, did you put the paint there?" Mr. Sanders asked.

Isiah shook his head. The Aldens all looked at Brett.

Brett's face turned red. "I did," he admitted. "I've been dressing up as a headless horseman and borrowing Domino. I used the paint and the glitter to make him black and frightening."

"Did you do all the other tricks too?" Henry asked. "The tube with the eyes in the woods?"

"Yes," Brett said. "And I hurt my wrist yesterday when I was trying to climb the tree."

"What about the fake worms and dirt in the cookie jar?" Jessie asked. "Did you do that too?"

He ducked his head. "I did that too. I'm very, very sorry."

"Brett, how could you?" Mr. Beekman was shocked and angry.

"I wanted the Vanderhoffs to sell their house so we could buy it. I don't always want to be a waiter."

"That's no excuse for all you've done," Mr. Beekman said. "Mr. Sanders could call the police. You've been stealing his horse."

Mr. Sanders sat down on a stool. "I can't say I understand exactly what's going on, but since the horse is back here in his stall, there's no need to call the police. He doesn't look like he's been harmed."

"Brett will pay you for the time he was riding him though, the regular rental fee." Mr. Beekman said.

"Well, right now I need something more than money. I could use more help mucking out these stalls. Especially since Isiah will be spending more time in New York City."

"I'll see that he's here whenever you need him." Mr. Beekman turned to Annika. "And he'll make it up to you too."

Before Annika could answer, her cell phone rang. She answered, and when she hung up a few moments later, she was smiling. "I can hardly believe it. That was Margot. They've been getting calls at the office from people wanting to go on the haunted ghost tour they've heard about. People who want to be scared! I guess I'll have to change my tours."

"I can help," Brett said. "I know that won't make up for all the tricks I played, but it will be a start. I'm good at thinking up ways to scare people."

"Yes, you are," Violet and Benny said together. Everyone laughed.

"I don't know." Annika frowned. "You'll have to stop being mean to Isiah."

"I will, I promise. And I'll think up tricks that not even the Aldens will be able to figure out."

"I wouldn't count on that," Mrs. Vanderhoff said. "I suspect Sleepy Hollow wouldn't be very spooky if the Aldens lived here. They'd solve all our hauntings and mysteries."

"We'd be happy to try," Jessie said.

Mr. Beekman looked at his watch. "Before the Aldens take on another mystery, I'd like you all to be my guests at the library dinner tonight. It's starting soon. Mr. Sanders and Isiah too. The Alden detectives deserve a feast after all their hard work."

"We did work hard, didn't we?" Benny said. "I knew there was a reason I'm so hungry. Let's go!"

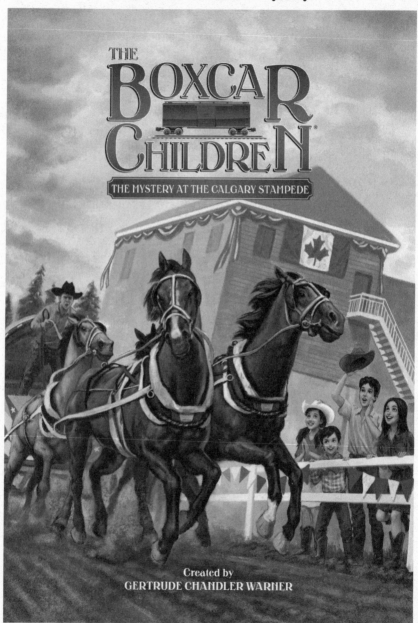

THE

BOXCAR CHILDREN

THE MYSTERY AT THE CALGARY STAMPEDE

Created by
GERTRUDE CHANDLER WARNER

PB ISBN: 9780807528419, $5.99

Judy's portrait. Henry thought that the man had been there for a while and that maybe he'd seen Judy give the pin to Daisy. The man stepped up to speak to Henry. "That's a special pin," he said in a low voice. "That piece would be a nice addition to the museum!" He explained, "I'm an amateur collector of Stampede memorabilia myself."

All the conversations stopped just then as Daisy noticed the man.

The man smiled and motioned to the painting. "Congratulations, ma'am," he said to Judy, "on your many accomplishments. And you, young girl"—he turned to Daisy—"are very lucky."

Daisy didn't seem to know what to say. Judy reached out to shake the man's hand, but he'd already turned away. "It's a beautiful pin," he said gazing at the portrait. "Not too many of them around. Hope you don't mind…" he said and took an old-fashioned camera from the big leather bag hanging from his shoulder and snapped a picture of the portrait.

Before anyone else could say anything, he walked away.

Suddenly Daisy looked anxious, but her aunt put an arm around her. "You'll be just fine. Look," Judy said, pointing to the Aldens. "My good friend is visiting with his grandchildren. They'll be staying with me."

"I hope you like Calgary," Daisy told them.

Benny beamed. "We will!" he said. "We can't wait to see your show!"

"Oh, it's not *my* show," said Daisy, her voice uneasy.

"You know," said her aunt, "I was going to wait until after dinner tonight but I think I'll give you my pin right here and now!"

Daisy was surprised. "Really?"

"I want you to have it," Judy told her. "You can wear it tomorrow night. I love the thought of my pin on the Stampede stage once again." She pulled a small velvet box from her pocket, took out the pin, and pinned it onto her niece's collar.

The Aldens clapped and Benny cheered. Daisy threw her arms around her aunt and gave her another hug.

As they were all talking, something caught Henry's eye. An older man was standing by rehearsal. But she doesn't know that I want to celebrate *her* too!

"Daisy is now a Young Canadian," she explained. "I have a feeling that this is the beginning of her own singing career. I'm so proud of her. Her first time performing on the Calgary stage is tomorrow night!"

Violet gave a squeak of excitement, and she turned to Grandfather. "Do we get to see the show?" she asked.

Before Grandfather could answer, Judy said, "Of course you do."

Just then a girl about Henry's age with bright red hair and a wide smile that matched Judy's ran up to give Judy a hug. "Auntie Judy!" she exclaimed.

Jessie knew this had to be Daisy.

Daisy saw the portrait of her aunt. "Oh my," she said. "It's beautiful!" She stepped back. "Look at that! The artist even put your pin on it."

"The pin you've wanted since you were a little girl," said Judy. "Now here you are, a Young Canadian yourself and ready for your first opening show!"

guess that was really *you*." The painting was a portrait of Judy standing in front of a concert marquee that read: *Judy Simon: Live at the Grand Ole Opry*.

Judy laughed. "It *is* very odd to see myself like that!"

Benny was staring hard at the portrait. "What is that pin you're wearing in the painting?"

"You have sharp eyes," said Judy. "That's my Young Canadian pin. That was given to me for being part of the singing and dancing troupe that performs every evening at the Stampede Grandstand Show. I was a Young Canadian for five years so they gave me a special pin with my name engraved on it!"

"Five years! That must have been a lot of work," said Jessie.

"It was," Judy said. "And it was how I got my start as a singer." She lowered her voice to a stage whisper. "The pin is the surprise I told you about. I'm going to give it to my niece Daisy. She's meeting us here to see my portrait for the first time. She had to miss the unveiling of the portrait because she was at grandfather brought you to our province of Alberta."

"In Canada a province is like a state," Jessie explained to her siblings.

"I'm so excited you're all finally here," Judy said. "Especially for Stampede time! Every July we open our city to the world for ten days. It's a giant party! We have cowboys from all over North America. We have chuckwagon races and young people exhibiting animals they've raised. We have a marvelous midway fair with rides and food—"

She noticed Benny's eyes widen. "Did I mention *food*?" Judy laughed. "You'll find some very strange foods at the Stampede."

Benny opened his mouth to ask her about the strange food, but she was already leading them into the museum.

"Look at this poster!" said Jessie. "It's from 2012 and says it's the hundredth anniversary of the Stampede!"

Grandfather stopped in front of a huge painting.

"Well, well," he said to Judy. "It's so lifelike that if you weren't standing in front of us, I'd

Grandfather pulled on the cord to let the driver know they were getting off the bus.

Violet pointed to another painted window. "Look—it says, 'Welcome to Cow Town.' Is there really a city with that name?"

Henry shook his head. "I think we're in the city of Calgary. Grandfather, you told us about it when you were telling us about your friend Judy. It's also called Cow Town, you said. And my guess is that it's Stampede time. Right?"

Grandfather smiled wide. "You're right, Henry! Cow Town Calgary, it is."

They'd come to a building with a sign that read *Glenbow Museum*. A woman was standing in front. She had a huge smile on her face and bright red hair that sat in a pile atop her head.

"Our Calgary Stampede is called the Greatest Outdoor Show on Earth," she said in a deep, rich voice. She must have overheard them. She put out her hand. "I'm your grandfather's friend, Judy Simon!"

She shook each of the Aldens' hands and chuckled. "I thought it was about time your

"So," said Henry as the plane taxied toward the airport, "where are we?"

Grandfather chuckled. "I'm going to let you guess." He led the way through the airport and onto a bus.

Half an hour later, Benny was kneeling on his seat, looking out the window. "All the windows of shops and restaurants and offices in this city are painted with cows and horses and cowboy hats and boots." He pointed to a revolving door in a tall building. "Look at that! It's painted like old-time Western saloon doors!"

GERTRUDE CHANDLER WARNER discovered when she was teaching that many readers who like an exciting story could find no books that were both easy and fun to read. She decided to try to meet this need, and her first book, *The Boxcar Children*, quickly proved she had succeeded.

Miss Warner drew on her own experiences to write the mystery. As a child she spent hours watching trains go by on the tracks opposite her family home. She often dreamed about what it would be like to set up housekeeping in a caboose or freight car—the situation the Alden children find themselves in.

While the mystery element is central to each of Miss Warner's books, she never thought of them as strictly juvenile mysteries. She liked to stress the Aldens' independence and resourcefulness and their solid New England devotion to using up and making do. The Aldens go about most of their adventures with as little adult supervision as possible—something else that delights young readers.

Miss Warner lived in Putnam, Connecticut, until her death in 1979. During her lifetime, she received hundreds of letters from girls and boys telling her how much they liked her books.

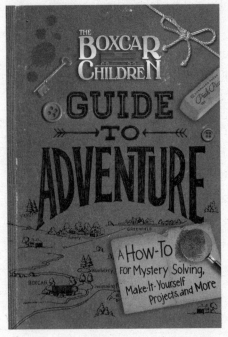